Drummer Girl

Drummer Girl

by
Hiba Masood

Illustrated by
Hoda Hadadi

DAYBREAK PRESS

First published in 2016

Drummer Girl by Hiba Masood and illustrated by Hoda Hadadi

For more information visit daybreakpress.rabata.org

Published by
Daybreak Press
Minneapolis, Minnesota

ISBN: 978-0-9906259-7-1
Library of Congress number: 2016941813

Typesetting and layout: www.scholarlytype.com

بِسْمِ ٱللَّهِ ٱلرَّحْمَٰنِ ٱلرَّحِيمِ

For my Baba

Many years ago in Istanbul, at the far end of Gul Pasha Caddesi, where the cobbled road dips towards the Sea of Marmara, there was a small white house with a brick-red roof.

If you ever walked by this house on a Friday evening, when the sun was setting and the neighbors were lighting their kitchen lanterns, you would hear an old woman singing softly to herself:

Why do you sleep, why do you sleep
Wake if you know what is better for you

Why do you sleep, why do you sleep
Your Lord, the Merciful, is waiting for you

If you followed the lilting melody and peeped inside the black iron gate of the small white house with the brick-red roof, you would see Grandma Najma sitting on the front steps.

Grandma Najma would look up at you questioningly. Her brown eyes, the exact shade of a *mabroor* date, would squint a little, but her strong, wrinkled hands would go on tapping the beat of her song against knees carefully hidden under the folds of her long red skirt.

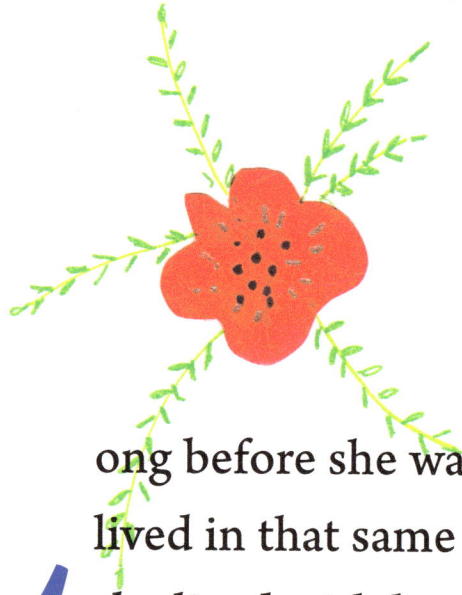

Long before she was Grandma Najma, she was simply Najma. She had lived in that same house since she was a little girl, but in those days she lived with her baba, her mama, and her two brothers. Najma went to school in the morning, and in the evening she helped her mama around the house. As she swept the earthen floors and washed the porcelain cups in which her baba drank his fragrant cardamom tea, she would sing:

Wake, o' believers, big and small
Your Lord is watchful over you all

Rise, o' believers, say in one rousing call
Ramadan Kareem! Ramadan Kareem!

6

ajma loved Ramadan. She loved searching the sky for the new moon with her baba and stringing up the *fanoos* lights. She loved wearing the special clothes sewn by her mama. She loved the fancy tea set that Mama would take out, with its tiny spoons that her brother would carefully shine, and the steaming bowls of *shorba* that they all had for *iftar*. She loved falling asleep to the sound of night prayers at the distant *masjid*. Most of all, she loved waking up before dawn as the *musaharati* passed through her street.

A *musaharati* is a special Ramadan drummer. He walks through the neighborhood in the hours before dawn, beating a drum and chanting special songs. He does this to wake all the sleeping people so that they may take *suhoor*, the pre-fast meal, and pray the *Fajr* prayer before the long day of fasting begins. A *musaharati* stands in front of each home and calls the people of that home by name.

Every night in Ramadan, Najma would hear her father's name being called out by the *musaharati* at their door:

Wake, o' Ali! Wake, o' household of Ali!
The time for the Lord's bounty is upon you!

For as long as Najma could remember, Ramadan had meant hearing the *musaharati*—the thump-thump-thump of his drum and the sing-song poetry of his melodious voice. And for as long as Najma could remember, she had carried a secret dream.

Najma wanted to be a *musaharati*!

Rise up from your beds, let sleep leave from you
Stand up in prayer, let your Lord be pleased with you

She would hum the tunes of the *musaharati* and imagine walking through the neighborhood waking up her friends and neighbors.

One day, when Najma was twelve years old and Ramadan preparations had begun, she went and sat on the floor by her baba. She put her head on his knee and he stroked her hair. "Yes, Najma? What is it that worries you?"

Najma took a deep breath and all the words spilled out of her. "Baba, I want to be the *musaharati* this year. I want to beat the drum and sing the verses and wake everyone for *suhoor*. My friend told me that Brother Yusuf, our neighborhood *musaharati*, is not feeling well and is looking for a replacement. I want to be his replacement. Please. This dream is calling to me, Baba. It has been calling to me for years."

Baba's hand stilled on her head and Najma held her breath. Would he be angry? Would he say she was being foolish? No woman had ever been a *musaharati* in her neighborhood. In fact, no woman had ever been a *musaharati* anywhere, as far as she knew. Najma looked up nervously. Baba's kind eyes met hers. He was not angry.

After a long time, Baba spoke. "You want to be the *musaharati*?"

"Yes, Baba," Najma whispered.

Baba tapped her gently on the nose and slowly smiled. "Well…I don't see why not."

Najma's heart leapt with joy. If Baba had spoken, then that was that. And do you know what? That *was* that. Her brothers said she was being silly. Her friends thought she had lost her mind. But Baba had spoken.

Like beads slipping by on a *tasbeeh*, the days passed and Ramadan came closer and closer.

"Girls can't be *musaharatis*!" someone said to Najma every day.

"Girls can be anything they like," Baba said to her every night.

Soon, Ramadan arrived. The curving silver crescent of the new moon had been seen and the neighbors called out joyous greetings to each other from their doors and windows, "Ramadan is here! Glad tidings for a wonderful month!"

That night, when her brothers had gone to bed, Najma put on her favorite long red skirt and wrapped her scarf around her. She took out the drum Baba had brought for her earlier, put on her gloves, and slipped out.

Najma and her baba walked through narrow alleys and twisting pathways, up and down the cobbled roads of their neighborhood. Najma's strong, clear voice rang out again and again through the night air. Her hands beat steadily on her drum, thump-thump-thump, as she and Baba paused outside the homes of their neighbors:

Wake up from your beds if you believe
The blessings of suhoor you must achieve

There's no time to sleep, no time to dream
Say it now with me: Ramadaaaan Kareeeeem!

Many people stepped out onto their balconies to watch. Was it really a *girl's* voice they had heard? Some laughed at Najma as she walked by. Others threw candy and sweets down to her, which she received with a shy nod.

When Najma and her baba had drummed at the doors of all the neighbors, they went home. Mama had their *suhoor* ready for them. Najma was hungry and tired. She ate quickly, prayed *Fajr*, and went to sleep for a long time.

While she slept, Najma had a beautiful dream. She saw herself walking with her drum down a long, winding path illuminated by lanterns of different colors and sizes. As she walked, she could hear the sound of many people reciting the Qur'an.

When she woke, Najma felt happy and peaceful inside. She felt sure she would be a good *musaharati* and that Allah was pleased with her.

That Ramadan, Najma and her baba spent all their nights the same way. They walked through the neighborhood and Najma sang out her verses and beat her drum. When the neighbors realized that Najma was coming out night after night, they no longer laughed or teased her. They grew to respect and love the brave, determined little girl who was waking them for the most important meal of their long Ramadan days. They invited her family to break the fast in their homes and proudly spoke of her in other neighborhoods.

For many years afterward, in that small Istanbul neighborhood at the end of Gul Pasha Caddesi, it was Najma who was the Ramadan *musaharati*. She was as much a part of her neighbors' Ramadan as their dates, their cardamom coffee, and their nightly prayers.

As the years passed, her baba began staying at home, and she would go alone or with her brothers. As more years passed, Najma's husband began walking with her. Later, her children walked with her. After that, her grandchildren.

When the time came that Grandma Najma's bones grew too tired for her to be a *musaharati* anymore, she gave her drum to her grandchildren and they carried on the noble family tradition she had set. But even then, every Ramadan evening, Grandma Najma would carefully put on her favorite long red skirt and wrap her shawl around her shoulders. She would sit on the steps of her small white house with the brick-red roof and gently tap her wrinkled hands against her knees, singing:

Why do you sleep, why do you sleep
Rise if you know what is better for you

Hurry and wake, His blessings to take
Your Lord, the Merciful, is waiting for you

Come sing with me, believers big and small
Say it together now, in one rousing call

Ramadan Kareem! Ramadan Kareem! Ramadan Kareem!

Author's Note

RAMADAN is the most special time of the Islamic calendar year. It is a month eagerly awaited for its festive atmosphere, rich traditions, and divine blessings. Every family has its own particular Ramadan culture, but Muslims all over the world are united in their desire to make Ramadan the most spiritually fruitful month of the year.

When I was a little girl, my baba used to tell me that when he was a little boy, the *musaharati* would walk through the neighborhood beating his drum to wake everyone for *suhoor*. Every night, as young boys, my baba and his brothers would sit on the roof, waiting for the *musaharati* to come by so they could greet him and then begin the morning meal.

In most places in the Muslim world, this tradition has faded away with the advent of new technologies—alarm clocks and smartphones are now in every home. But even today, in smaller neighborhoods in places as varied as Pakistan, Syria, Turkey, and Egypt, the *musaharati* still walks the streets every night, beating his drum—a beloved figure and a symbol of Ramadan.

One Ramadan, I remembered my baba's story and began researching this tradition for a book. During my research, I chanced upon the true account of a woman *musaharati* in Cairo who became her family's breadwinner after her husband died. She held multiple jobs to generate enough income to raise her children, and one of them was this rich Ramadan tradition of walking through the streets beating a drum. Her story captured my imagination, and *Drummer Girl* was born.

Terms

Iftar The meal at the setting of the sun, which breaks the fast. It is part of the Prophetic tradition to begin this meal with a date.

Fajr One of the five daily prayers for Muslims. Fajr is the dawn prayer, which in Ramadan also marks the beginning of the day's fast.

Fanoos Light or lantern, widely associated with Ramadan.

Mabroor A species of date.

Maghrib One of the five daily prayers for Muslims. Maghrib is the sunset prayer, which in Ramadan marks the end of the day's fast.

Masjid The Arabic term for mosque, which is the place Muslims gather to pray.

Shorba A soup made of varied ingredients such as lentils, broth, wheat, and barley. It is a typical Ramadan dish in many parts of the world.

Suhoor The pre-dawn meal, consumed before the fasting day commences.

Tasbeeh Muslim prayer beads.

About the Author

HIBA MASOOD is a Canadian-Pakistani writer, storyteller, and speaker. Apart from running her wildly popular Facebook page (Drama Mama), she is also a columnist for Muslim Matters. Currently based in Karachi, Hiba runs Happy Place, an enrichment center for women and kids, where she holds story, art and yoga sessions centered around her primary passion, children's literature. Hiba is also a founding partner of Veritas Learning Circle, Pakistan's first Waldorf-inspired early education school. She is the author of *Aiza and Alina*, a story of friendship and Down Syndrome, which she wrote for use in inclusive education programs across Pakistan.

Drummer Girl is Hiba's second book. As an uplifting story about empowered women and a supportive father, this book encapsulates her mission in life: to encourage women to become their best, most radiant selves and to celebrate everyone who helps them in this essential journey.

About the Illustrator

HODA HADADI is an award-winning illustrator, painter, poet, and writer. Since earning her BA in Graphic Design from the University of Art, Tehran, she has published more than 50 books in Iran, the United States, France, Italy, Denmark, Japan, China, the United Arab Emirates, and more.

Among her awards and prizes are the Best of Arabic Books Award for Children, 2015 (Bahrain); the New Horizons Award of Bologna, 2010 (Italy); Third Prize at the Teatro Festival, 2008 (Italy); The Golden Plaque of BIB, 2007 (Slovakia); Second Prize of Katha, 2005 (India); First Prize at the Kanoon Book Festival, 2005 (Iran); and the NOMA Encouragement Prize, 2002 & 2008 (Japan).

رباطة شروق

About the Press

DAYBREAK PRESS is the publishing arm of Rabata, an international organization
dedicated to promoting positive cultural change through creative
educational experiences. Daybreak is committed to publishing
female scholars, activists and authors in the genres of poetry,
fiction, non-fiction and academic works. For
more information, please visit
rabata.org/daybreakpress.